A Boy's Life of Napoleon

Fiction by Alden Nowlan

The Wanton Troopers (1988)
Will Ye Let the Mummers In? (1984)
Various Persons Named Kevin O'Brien (1973)
Miracle at Indian River (1968)

ALDEN NOWLAN

A Boy's Life of Napoleon

GOOSE LANE EDITIONS

"A Boy's Life of Napoleon" was originally published
as the first three chapters of Alden Nowlan's
1988 novel, *The Wanton Troopers*,
published by Goose Lane Editions.

1

It was raining so hard that Kevin thought God must have torn a hole in the sky and let all of the rivers of heaven spill upon earth. The cold spring rain hit the roof with the force of gravel, rattled down the walls, and splashed black and silver against the tawny window panes. It felt good to be in the house, safe in the sleepy warmth and lamp glow of the kitchen, breathing the soporific aromas of smouldering millwood and burning kerosene.

A clock ticked on the shelf above the pantry door, scarcely audible above the strident clatter of the storm. The kerosene lamps, one on the table by the window and the other on a shelf above the cot, threw out inverted cones of orange-yellow light that shimmered until they were dissolved by the shadows in the corners of the room. On the ceiling above each lamp, there whirled a golden halo.

His mother had set the wash tub in front of the stove. She took buckets of cold water from under the sink and emptied them into the tub, then added hot water from a pan boiling on the stove. Steam rose in sibilant clouds, glistening ghostly as it was absorbed by the dry air.

"Come, Scampi," his mother said.

This was her private name for him. He stood on a towel while she undressed him. His body relaxed into will-lessness, went limp as she removed the shirt his grandmother had made for him from bleached-out flour bags. He liked the way in which the room became a violent ferment of darkness and light while the shirt was being pulled over his eyes. And he liked her hands, their deft union of firmness and gentleness.

His father dozed on the cot. His grandmother had long since gone to bed. This was a private moment, shared only by him and his mother. He never loved her so much as when she bathed him and readied him for bed.

Outside, over the oozing, dun-coloured fields, down the overflowing creek, through the gurgling swamps, and across the cedared hills, the wind howled like a drowning beast. Inside, there was warmth and light and the music of his mother's hands on his body.

She undid buckles and buttons and let his denim shorts slide down his legs. From May to November, he never wore underwear. He stepped out of the ring of cloth around his ankles and into the tub, recoiling as the cold rim touched his back. He leaned forward, away from the ring of cold.

Now, there was the clean, acid smell of soap in his nostrils, the foam and film of soap in his hair and across his shoulders and down his back. He closed his eyes and sank into little-boy inertia, every muscle dormant, every cell in his brain passive and inert.

Around his thighs, hips, and belly, the water's warmth coaxed the energy out of his every pore. His knees and chest were prickled by the sharper heat of the stove, little slivers of heat shooting into his flesh.

She rubbed a washcloth over his face. He drew back a little as the soap bit his eyes and nostrils. She put her hand against the back of his head and made him keep still — and he liked the peremptoriness of her gestures. Like the stinging needles from the stove, this mild discomfort accentuated their intimacy, made it more sweet.

He might have been a part of her body. She washed him as she washed her own hands. He was, all of him, hers: not the smallest part of him belonged any longer to himself. And in this surrender, there was a pervasive peace, an ecstasy of negation.

She kneaded suds into the soft fat of his belly, and he sank into the weightless dimension between wakefulness and sleep. When she made him stand up, it was as though he were coming awake.

Wind still pounded the house; rain was a rumbling landslide on the roof. With each gust, the lamp by the window flickered and the door shook on its rusty hinges. But he was only dimly aware of these things. She scrubbed his legs, rubbing his knees until they stung, the pressure of her hands softening as they ran up and down his thighs, tickling him so that he writhed and giggled. On the cot, his father — that man of ironwood and axe blades — continued to sleep. Upstairs, his grandmother was dreaming of crowns and trumpets and of the golden streets of Jerusalem. When his mother dried him with a towel made from a flour bag, she stroked him so briskly his body glowed as though it had become phosphorescent with sensuous fire.

Finishing, she draped the towel around his hips, like a loincloth.

"Me Jane. You Tarzan," she laughed.

Their communion of warmth had ended. Now, as he always did at such times, he felt a feverish desire for sound and action. He threw his arms around her and squeezed, exerting all his strength.

"Ohhhhh! You're hurting me!" she cried in mock pain.

"I'm the king of the great bull apes!" he boasted. "You wanta hear me give the cry of the great bull apes, Mummy?"

The previous fall, they had gone to the motion picture house in Larchmont, and ever since, Tarzan and Jane had been a game between them.

"Oh! You forgot! I'm not Mummy, I'm Jane!"

"Sure! You Jane! Me Tarzan!"

He threw back his head and howled until he was out of breath. She laughed again and slapped his posterior playfully.

His father snorted, shook himself, and sat up on the side of the cot. Rubbing his eyes, he glared at them angrily.

"For Chrissakes, Kevin, do yuh have tuh make so damn much noise!" he roared.

Kevin blushed and stared at the floor. Water that had dripped from his body as he stepped out of the tub lay in the little valleys in the warped linoleum.

"Yer gittin' too big tuh act like a baby," his father growled. He fumbled in the pockets of his jeans, found tobacco and papers, and began rolling a cigarette.

"Yessir," Kevin mumbled.

Shrinking with shame and self-contempt, he thought of how pitiful was his own skinny, almost hairless body in comparison with that of his father. Judd O'Brien's arms were bludgeons, and his horny, yellow fingernails reminded Kevin of hooves.

"Come to bed, Scampi," his mother said.

She laid her hand on his shoulder. With a scowl of irritation, he drew away. He hated her when she caressed him before his father, for he knew that Judd despised all caresses as symptoms of weakness. Even now, so it seemed to Kevin, Judd eyed him with undisguised contempt.

She took his shoulder again. This time her fingers dug into his flesh. He knew that she had sensed the reason for his withdrawal and that she resented it.

"Come to bed, Scampi," she commanded him.

She took the lamp from the shelf and, carrying it in front of her and above her head, led Kevin to his room at the other end of the house.

Setting the lamp on a chair by his bed, she helped him into the worn-out shirt of his father's that he wore as a nightdress. The air in this room smelled vaguely stale. It was strange how the odour of a room indicated the amount it was used. The air here contained just a hint of the staleness to be found in the unfurnished rooms upstairs.

He wiggled under the patchwork quilts, under the grey wool blankets that his uncle Kaye had stolen from the bunkhouse of the last sawmill in which he had worked. His mother put the lamp on the floor and sat in the chair by his pillow. At this end of the house, the storm was muted; water running from the eaves splashed almost gently against the window.

She leaned over him, and again he inhaled the aura of her presence: the scent of her perfume that always reminded him of wintergreen and lilacs; the pungent, comfortable odour of her body, the smell of grease and cooking oils and sweat.

"Do you love me, Mummy?"

This was the beginning of a nightly ritual.

"Yes, sweetheart, I love you."

"How much do you love me, Mummy?"

"Oh, I love you a thousand million bushels, sweetikins, a thousand million bushels."

"I love you too, Mummy."

The words, spoken in a drowsy monotone, were, in reality, not words at all, but sound units in a charm. They were *abracadabra,* a charm against the dark powers of the night.

"Let's say our prayers now, Scampi."

"Yeah."

He chanted, running syllables together so that the prayer was broken, not by words, but by the rhythm of his breath.

Now I lay me down to sleep,
I pray the Lord my soul to keep.
If I should die before I wake,
I pray the Lord my soul to take.
God bless Mummy and Daddy,
and Uncle Kaye, and Grammie O'Brien,
and God bless everybody.

2

The morning was bright and boundless, the air electric with that sense of freedom, of infinite distances and open spaces, that comes on a sunlit morning following a rain. Kevin had breakfasted on milk, toast, and porridge flavoured with molasses. Now he was walking down the gravelled road, toward the schoolhouse.

He kept to the soft shoulder of the road, where there was no gravel to sting his bare feet. The odour of the mud made him think of the strangely pleasant stink of horse manure and fresh-ploughed earth. A purple mist hung low over the fields and drifted lazily through the jungle of alders, willows, and mullein lining the overflowing ditches. Little beads of moisture adhered to the almost invisible hair on his legs, chilling him.

From the thickets came the shrill, toy-like song of the wood pewee and the raucous cry of the red-winged blackbird. Over the hill, on the intervals beyond the railroad track, great flocks of crows were cawing. Kevin noted that each crow cawed three times. Caw! Caw! Caw! He could not remember ever having noticed this before. Caw! Caw! Caw! Three caws each time. Never more, never less.

Reflected sunlight glistened on daisies, dandelions, and buttercups. The rain had raked petals from the wild rose bushes and many of them had been blown on the coarse gravel, where they lay, soggy but still delicate and velvety.

He came to a place where the road was bounded on both sides by barriers of spruce, stunted pine, and fir. It was colder here, because the trees shut out the heat of the sun, and the trees were dark; even at noon, all evergreens seemed to be dreaming of the haunted darkness of midnight.

Coming out of the woods, he passed the sawmill. This place both attracted and frightened him. The steam engine pulsed with ferocious, relentless power, pounding until the long, low, shed-like building shook on its log foundations. At intervals, the big saw emitted its scream of agony and triumph: the agony of the cleanly sliced log, the triumph of the luminous disc and its invisible, irresistible teeth.

There were five saws in the mill, Kevin knew. He had gone there many times, carrying tobacco or a lunch to his father. The biggest saw was called the splitter and Judd was known as the splitterman. When a slab dropped from the log carriage, Judd seized it and hurled it down the rollers to the slab sawyer. When a board fell free, he grasped it and, half-turning, threw it on a rack, from which it was taken by the edgerman. Judd had worked in the mill every summer since his fourteenth birthday.

The slab saw hung between two hinged beams. Cutting a slab into stovewood lengths, the slab sawyer gripped a metal bar attached to the beam and jerked the saw toward him, steadying the slab with his other hand. Twice in the years that Kevin could remember, slab sawyers had lost fingers, and once the swinging blade had ripped off a man's hand...

The edgerman trimmed the strips of bark from the edges of the boards. He stood about twelve feet from his small, twin saws and worked them with a long wooden lever. The saws could be moved in accordance with the width of the board. As each board was thrown, screeching, from the jaws of the edger, it was grasped by the trimmerman, whose saw tore off its ragged ends.

When these saws were working at full speed, they ceased to be substantial, metal things and became rings of nebulous, convulsive light. Kevin could remember moments in which he could hardly resist an urge to thrust his hand into one of these luminous rings. There had been times when his desire had become so strong that he had felt his stomach contract in fear as he turned away. He wondered if the men who worked in the mill ever felt tempted to throw themselves into these hypnotic whirlpools. In the twenty-five years that his father had worked at the mill, three men had been killed.

Steam billowed from the great, guy-wired stack and spurted from the exhaust pipe over the well. The saliva-light odour of steam mingled with the acrid tang of green sawdust. The millyard was full of men, all of them working furiously with logs and lumber. Even Stingle, who sometimes got drunk with Kevin's father, walked ahead of his team of yellow oxen, twirling his black whip over his head. The oxen had gentle eyes in their huge, stupid heads. Zombie-like, they plodded behind their driver, their heads bent low under the red yoke with its leather straps studded with brass and copper rivets, red knobs attached to the tips of their inward-curving yellow horns.

The oxen hauled a drag, called a log boat. All of the oxen in the world were named Broad, Bright, Star, Lion, Buck, or Brown. Horses, Kevin liked and sometimes feared; for these beasts, he felt only pity. No matter how often it was beaten, a horse retained a little glimmering spark of wildness. When let out to pasture on Sunday, even the old, sway-backed nag that pulled the sawdust cart would sometimes toss her head and neigh like a high-spirited colt. Kevin feared the teeth and hooves of horses, but something in him responded to the secret light he saw in their eyes, the freedom and grace that could never be wholly destroyed by work or punishment but ended only with death, because its life was inseparable from the life of their bodies.

The oxen were strong, but their strength was as lifeless as that of the steam engine. They did not husband their strength, as horses often did. When yoked to a load, they pulled as hard as they could from the first, and they continued to exert all their strength until they were halted by their teamster. Under the lash, a horse would cringe or strike out with its hooves; an ox accepted pain as stolidly as it accepted changes in the weather.

"Hello, Mister Man," Eben Stingle said.

"Hi."

"If yuh don't hurry, yer gonna be late for school. Then, most likely, yuh'll git stood in the corner."

Eben laughed, revealing tobacco-stained false teeth. Kevin grinned. He thought the joke inane, like most of the things men said to boys. But he always grinned when anyone smiled at him. The response came instinctively, and he was hardly aware of it.

Beyond the mill, the road re-entered the woods. Poplar, maple, birch, and cedar grew here, crowded so close together that they sucked the life from one another's roots. The trunks of these trees were so small that Kevin could have spanned them with his hands, but they grew to great heights, stretching upwards toward the sun.

The schoolhouse was about a mile from Kevin's house. He turned into the yard now. The tin-roofed, whitewashed building sat in the centre of a half-acre field, surrounded by flat and almost lifeless grass. A ragged and faded Union Jack hung limp from a pole opposite the door. Little crayon sketches of animals were pasted to the foggy glass of the windows. Approaching the open door to the porch, Kevin felt his stomach tie itself into a familiar giddy knot, his throat throb with the raw dryness of fear.

He entered the semidarkness of the porch. Half a dozen boys lounged against walls studded with coat hooks. Among them were two husky fifteen-year-olds in Grade VI: Riff Wingate, whose grin revealed a mouthful of broken, yellow teeth and whose breath stank of decay, and Harold Winthrop, whose face was pocked with feverish, red pimples and who liked to boast of the things that he had done to girls. To Riff and Harold, school was a ribald joke. Next summer, they would be peeling pulp or sawing slabs at the mill.

"Well, if it ain't Key-von!" Riff laughed.

Kevin reached for the knob of the inner door. Lifting his leg lazily, Harold barred his way.

"What's yer hurry, Key-von? Don't yuh like the company?" Harold smirked.

Ashen-faced, his hands by his sides, Kevin said nothing. Av Farmer stepped forward, a pudgy, fox-eyed boy of about Kevin's age. Kevin's terror of this boy was so abject that he could not muster sufficient pride to hate him.

Harold, Riff, and the others pressed close, grinning, their eyes bright with anticipation.

"The man spoke tuh yuh, Key-von," Av leered. "The cat got yer tongue or somethin'?"

"Mebbe he ain't learnt tuh talk yet," Alton Stacey guffawed.

Women said of Alton that he was pretty enough to be a girl. But his cunning had saved him from Riff and Harold. He had come to Lockhartville from Ontario, and he had cultivated the reputation of a sophisticate, a reputation he had enhanced by teaching Riff and Harold to shoot craps in the woodshed behind the schoolhouse. In these games, Alton invariably lost, and neither Riff nor Harold ever taunted him because of his resemblance to a girl.

"Show Daddy if the cat's got yer tongue!" Av demanded. He grabbed Kevin's collar and shoved him against the door. "Come on now, show Daddy!" The others giggled.

Kevin went limp. His paralysis was too negative a thing to be described as fear. His blood was water, his heart and brain ash. All feeling was dead. The room was a vibrating blur.

"Show Daddy, Key-von!"

Idiotically, he stuck out his tongue. The boys howled and danced with excitement. Kevin wished that he could sink through the floor, sink to the dark centre of the earth and cower there forever.

"Key-von's got a tongue! Cat didn't git it, after all!" Av shrieked.

"Did yuh see that! Did yuh see what Av done!" Riff was almost hysterical with joy.

Av reached out, grabbed Kevin's nose with one hand and his chin with the other, yanked his mouth open.

"Yessir, he's got a tongue!"

"Key-von's got a tongue!"

Mercifully, the bell rang. Av threw Kevin aside like a worn-out toy. The boys brushed past, elbowing him. Blindly, he stumbled after them into the classroom.

Kevin believed that every one of these boys was stronger, tougher, and braver than he. Secretly, he envied their courage and strength and wanted to be like them. But he consoled himself by the conviction that when they grew up they would be only pulp peelers and mill hands. They would live all their lives in Lockhartville, fenced in forests and rivers, and at last they would die here and be buried in the cemetery behind the Anglican church. But he — ah, he would be a lawyer, a doctor, a member of parliament, and one day he would come back here, wearing a black suit and a shining white shirt, and then he would spit in their eyes! And, in thinking this, his eyes and mouth took on that insolent, faintly contemptuous look that made them hate him.

Thirty children, ranging in age from six to fifteen, were seated at three rows of desks. The desks and seats in each row, made of scarred wood and rusting metal, were linked together so that they reminded Kevin of the cars in a train. Frayed canvas maps, rolled up like scrolls, hung over each of the three blackboards. The air was heavy with the smell of chalk, soap, sweat, and the stale crumbs of yesterday's sandwiches.

Miss Roache, the teacher, sat facing the children from behind her desk at the front of the room. Kevin slid into the seat that he shared with Alton Stacey.

"Good morning, class," Miss Roache enunciated.

"Good morning, Miss Roache," they chanted.

Kevin never joined in such chants. He thought the meaningless singsong sounded idiotic. The children used a peculiar tone when they spoke in school, an undulating croon with the emphasis falling in unexpected places. It was as if they were reading words in a language they could not understand.

"Class, stand," said Miss Roache.

With a clatter, the children got to their feet. They all of them derived a bit of sly excitement from this business of getting up and sitting down. The boys rattled the metal parts of their desks, the cotton dresses of the girls rustled like a windswept grain field.

O Canada
Our home and native land,
True patriot love,
In all thy sons command!
With glowing hearts, we see thee rise,
The true north, strong and free,
And stand on guard, O Canada!
We stand on guard for thee!

The older girls did most of the singing. Their voices, a little spiteful with self-conscious assurance, rang out above the drone of the younger children. The older boys grinned and were silent.

"We will bow our heads in prayer."

Again the mindless, undulating croon:

Our Father, which art in heaven,
hallowed be Thy name,
Thy kingdom come, Thy will be done,
on earth, as it is in heaven.
Give us this day our daily bread
and forgive us our trespasses
as we forgive those who trespass against us,
and lead us not into temptation,
but deliver us from evil,
for Thine is the kingdom and the power
and the glory,
forever and ever. Amen.

"Class, be seated."

There was another clatter and rustle, another little thrill of excitement and derision, as they resumed their seats.

"Now we shall take our Testaments and have our morning Bible reading."

Kevin took the small black book from the niche in his desk. His paralysis was lifting now. He was settling into the inertia of the school day.

Sunlight poured through the eastern windows, changing the crayon animals on the glass into grotesque abstractions. Miss Roache read aloud while the children stared with unfocused eyes at the books that lay open before them.

> *Follow after charity and desire spiritual gifts, but rather that ye may prophesy. For he that speaketh in an unknown tongue speaketh not unto man, but unto God, for no man understandeth him; howbeit in the spirit, he speaketh mysteries…*

The voice droned on. Kevin's body became a vegetable. The children might have been so many carrots and turnips, propped up in their seats.

Therefore, if I know not the meaning of the voice, I shall be unto him that speaketh a barbarian, and he that speaketh shall be a barbarian unto me. Therefore, let him that speaketh in an unknown tongue pray that he may interpret...

He stared at Miss Roache, observing that she nodded as she read, her head bobbing up and down. She reminded him of a dog eating: the little, furtive sideways glances she cast when she raised her head. He remembered how she had wept the previous winter when some of the big boys, led by Harold and Riff, threw snowballs through the open door and onto the stove. The steam had swirled up like fog, and Miss Roache had wept and sent the children home. That day, Kevin had wanted to weep with her. He had wanted to go to her and say that it didn't matter, that Riff and Harold were fools, that she should not let them hurt her. But, of course, he had done nothing of the kind. And the next day, she had beaten little Normie Fenton, the smallest and shyest boy in the school, until his hands were red with blood…

> *Brethren, be not children in understanding; howbeit in malice ye be children, but in understanding be men… But if there be no interpreter let him keep silence in the church; and let him speak to himself and to God…*

She shut the book with a gesture of relief and finality. A little ripple of movement swept from child to child, like a ripple on the surface of water.

"Current events," Miss Roache said, as she dropped the book in the drawer of her desk.

Every morning, Miss Roache talked for fifteen

minutes on world affairs. To most of the children, these events were less real than the incidents in radio serials and comic books. Often, when asked to provide some news item for this period, the younger children related something that had transpired in *Buck Rogers*, *Superman*, or *Mandrake the Magician*. But, in listening to Miss Roache tell of the horrors taking place in the great world beyond the creek and the cedared hills, the world beyond Larchmont, beyond even Halifax, Kevin decided that this world, for all of its superficial foreignness, was in most ways only an extension of the world of his father and the mill.

Today, Miss Roache talked about Hitler, about his imminent capture and about the punishment that should be meted out to him. Kevin shuddered when she said it had been proposed that Hitler should be killed slowly with knives, a bit of his flesh being cut away each day. During the Bible reading, Miss Roache's voice had been a dull monotone; now it became shrill and emphatic.

She said that she considered the death with knives too merciful. Hitler should be locked up in a cage and carried all over the world, so that persons everywhere could come and spit on him. He should be fed pig feed, but only enough to keep him alive, because if he were allowed to die, he would be no longer capable of suffering. In the cage, he might survive for years, and in time, he could be brought to the little hamlets on the back roads, to places like Lockhartville... And every night he could be burnt with hot irons and beaten with whips, and the greatest doctors in the world would be on hand to see that he did not die.

Having heard Miss Roache deliver such monologues every morning for more than a year, Kevin had long ago decided that he sympathized with Hitler. In his pictures and especially in the caricatures that Miss Roache tore out of the Halifax newspapers and showed to the children, the tousle-haired, toothbrush-moustached man looked funny and pitiful. He made Kevin think of Wallie, the half-witted hired man at the Mosher farm. When Kevin saw Wallie he did not know whether to laugh or to cry. He felt the same indecision when he saw Miss Roache's cartoons of Hitler.

If they ever bring him to Lockhartville, I'll help him get away from them, Kevin vowed silently. For a little while each morning, Kevin was a dedicated Nazi. He wished he dare leap into the aisle, throw up his arm in a salute, and shout, Heil Hitler!

3

Kevin decided that when he grew up he would be king of Nicaragua. For months, he had been fascinated by the idea of becoming a king. From the little glassed-in bookcase that composed the school library, he had taken a book entitled *A Boy's Life of Napoleon*. The book fired his imagination. He decided that when he became a man, he too would make himself a master of men and empires.

Searching through an atlas for a likely country, he regretfully abandoned France, Spain, Germany, and Italy as too large and powerful. He doubted his ability to enlist sufficient volunteers to overthrow their governments. Finally, he chose Nicaragua, a tiny, purple blotch on the map. Yes, he would make himself ruler of Nicaragua. In his exercise books, he drew up time schedules and plans of campaign, fording rivers with a movement of his pencil, eliminating frontiers with a swipe of an eraser. In 1953, when he was twenty, he would raise an army of freebooters — perhaps one hundred men. They would seize a ship and sail to the Caribbean. In 1954, he would be crowned king. His Majesty Kevin I, by the Grace of God and the Constitution of the Kingdom, Commander-in-Chief and King of Nicaragua. Then, perhaps in 1955, he would invade Honduras and annex it to his domain. In 1957, he would plant his flag in El Salvador. In 1958, he would lead his troops into the capital city of Guatemala. By 1960, he would be Emperor of Central America.

With wax crayons, he made designs for flags, settling finally on a golden cross with a golden circle on a field of white. And he invented names for ships and regiments, pages of them. He would christen his first battleship *El Gringo*, and his personal bodyguards, whose uniform, which he spent an entire evening designing, bore a strong resemblance to the garb of a guardsman as depicted in *A Boy's Life of Napoleon*, would be known as King Kevin's Royal Hussars.

He supposed he would have to marry. Kings needed sons to continue their dynasties. And Princess Margaret Rose was only a little older than he... Then he remembered that Napoleon had divorced Josephine because she could not provide him with an heir. This puzzled him. He asked his mother: "Why couldn't Josephine have any children, Mummy?"

"Josephine who, sweetikins?"

"You know, Josephine, the one that married Napoleon."

Laughing, Mary threw her arms around him. She slid her hand inside the back of his shirt and ran her fingers up and down the little bumps in his spine. This was one of her favourite ways of caressing him.

"Oh, Scampi darling, you ask the craziest questions!"

He drew away sulkily. "I don't see nothin' crazy about that."

"No, it isn't really crazy. Just funny, sort of. But I don't know, lamb. I really don't know why Josephine couldn't have children. I suppose someday you'll find out all about it. When Mummy's little sugar baby gets to be a man, he's going to know all sorts of wonderful things."

Grandmother O'Brien spoke from her rocker, beneath the clock shelf. "Yer spoilin' the boy, Mary. Yer spoilin' the boy with yer foolishness."

Mary stroked Kevin under the chin and winked at him.

"We're poor people," Grandmother O'Brien said. "It ain't fittin' fer people like us tuh put on airs."

Mary winked at Kevin again.

Grandmother O'Brien said this often, to rebuke what she called the false pride of Kevin and his mother. "People like us should be willin' tuh take what's handed out tuh us. We're poor as dirt and allus will be. Puttin' on high and mighty airs ain't gonna change things none."

To ease the perpetual pain in her stomach, Martha O'Brien held a brick, heated on top of the stove and wrapped in an old wool sock, against her waist. She lived on crackers soaked in milk until they'd become an oozing pulp, but her soul was nourished on the flesh offered in sacrifice to the God of Abraham and of Isaac and of Jacob.

"The O'Briens has allus been poor, boy. But they allus knew their place. And they was allus willin' tuh work. The same with my people, the Havelocks; when a man hired a Havelock he knowed he was a-gonna git a day's work outta him. Yuh never caught a Havelock givin' hisself no stud-horse airs. They knew what they was and they never pretended tuh be nothin' else. I don't like that false pride I see in yuh, boy."

"Oh, my goodness, Grammie! Scampi just asked a simple little question!" Mary's voice rose in irritation.

Martha adjusted the pin in her black, bowl-shaped hairdo. "Mark my words, Mary, yer a-spoilin' that boy. Children should be seen and not heard, I allus say, children should be seen and not heard." Rocking complacently, she looked at Kevin with undisguised disapproval. "If that was my boy I'd Josephine him! I'd Josephine him out in the garden with a hoe. There's work tuh be done here. Ain't no earthly use of Judd workin' his heart out every night after he comes home from the mill. Put that boy out in the garden. Put him tuh work around the barn. He's big enough tuh work if he's ever gonna be!"

"Oh, Grammie, Scampi is only a baby. Things were different when you were young. You don't realize that, Grammie."

"I realize a long-legged cockalorum like that one should be doin' his share of work around the place instead of askin' questions about women havin' children."

Mary drew Kevin's face against her breast. "When Scampi grows up, he's going to work with his brain. His hands are going to be soft as a girl's — like the hands of the men who work in offices and stores in Larchmont. When he's a man, my baby is going to have nice, soft, pink hands just like he has now. You wait and see."

"Eh!" This sound, half snort and half grunt, was Martha's way of dismissing them as hopeless. She rocked vigorously, hugging her brick.

There was nothing that Kevin found more frustrating than his grandmother's sermons on the certainty of poverty and the duty of humility before one's betters. He writhed in vexation when she told him, as she often did, that within four years he would be working in the mill. He hated her for the grim satisfaction he detected in her voice. And his hate was made more vicious by the thought that she was probably right in her prediction.

Martha did not undress at night. She lay fully clothed on her bed, and when the pain became unbearable she came downstairs and heated bricks. Then, in the darkness, with the brick clutched to her belly, she rocked and sang hymns. Often, Kevin awoke and heard her voice rise like the cry of a ghost in the darkness at the other end of the house.

This was the hymn that she most often sang:

There is a fountain filled with blood,
Drawn from Emmanuel's veins,
And sinners plunged beneath that flood
Lose all their guilty stains.

E'er since by faith I saw that stream
Thy flowing did supply,
Redeeming love has been my theme
And shall be till I die.

ALDEN NOWLAN is widely recognized as one of the most brilliant and accessible voices to emerge in Canadian poetry. Born in Nova Scotia in 1933, Nowlan moved to Hartland, New Brunswick, when he was nineteen, where he was a reporter, editor, and general facilitator of the *Hartland Observer*. In 1963 Nowlan went to the *Telegraph Journal* where he worked as a reporter, night news editor, and subsequently a weekly columnist. Publishing his first book of poetry, *The Rose and the Puritan*, in 1958, with Fiddlehead Poetry Books, he went on to write poetry, fiction, non-fiction, and stage and television plays. He was Writer-in-Residence at the University of New Brunswick from 1968 until his death in June 1983. Over his lifetime he won numerous awards and accolades including the Governor General's Award for Poetry (*Bread, Wine and Salt*), a Guggenheim Fellowship, and two honorary degrees.

Copyright © 1988, 2009, 2014 by the Estate of Alden Nowlan.

All rights reserved. No part of this work may be reproduced or used in any form or by any means, electronic or mechanical, including photocopying, recording or any retrieval system, without the prior written permission of the publisher or a licence from the Canadian Copyright Licensing Agency (Access Copyright). To contact Access Copyright, visit www.accesscopyright.ca or call 1-800-893-5777.

Series edited by Martin James Ainsley.
Cover and series design by Chris Tompkins.
Art direction and page design by Julie Scriver.
Printed in Canada.
10 9 8 7 6 5 4 3 2 1

Library and Archives Canada Cataloguing in Publication

    Six@sixty / edited by Martin James Ainsley.

Short stories compiled to commemorate Goose Lane's sixtieth anniversary.
    1. A boy's life of Napoleon / Alden Nowlan.
Issued in print and electronic formats.
ISBN 978-0-86492-853-5 (set : pbk.).— ISBN 978-0-86492-793-4 (set : epub).—
ISBN 978-0-86492-857-3 (v. 1 : pbk.).— ISBN 978-0-86492-732-3 (v. 1 : epub).

    1. Ainsley, Martin James, 1969-, editor. II. Nowlan, Alden, 1933-1983.
Boy's life of Napoleon

PS8321.S59 2014   C813'.010806   C2014-902978-0
                                                                C2014-903186-6

Goose Lane Editions acknowledges the generous support of the Canada Council for the Arts, the Government of Canada through the Canada Book Fund (CBF), and the Government of New Brunswick through the Department of Tourism, Heritage, and Culture.

Goose Lane Editions
500 Beaverbrook Court, Suite 330
Fredericton, New Brunswick
CANADA E3B 5X4
www.gooselane.com

This book, typeset in Minion Pro
and Gill Sans, was printed and bound in Canada by
Friesens in Altona, Manitoba, on 55 lb. Rolland Enviro
100 FSC Natural Antique.